My Teacher Turns into a

TYRANNOSAURUS

Kim Caraher

Illustrated by Robert Dickins

sundance

Supa
DOOPERS

For information regarding permission, write to:
Sundance Publishing
234 Taylor Street
Littleton, MA 01460

Published by
Sundance Publishing
234 Taylor Street
Littleton, MA 01460

First published 1996 by
Addison Wesley Longman Australia Pty Limited
95 Coventry Street
South Melbourne 3205 Australia
Exclusive United States Distribution: Sundance Publishing

ISBN 0-7608-0770-1

Printed In Canada

J SUP

CONTENTS

To Marion and Stephen

1

Meet the Beast

I have a big problem with my new school. Actually, three big problems.

To get to school I have to get past a Beast, and three Vampires, and when I get there I'm likely to find a Tyrannosaurus.

Pretty tough, hey? Let me tell you about it.

When I start out, the tree-lined street looks peaceful. The birds are singing happily. The world is okay.

Then I reach that horrible, horrifying house.
It looks like most of the others, but it is haunted
by a Beast thirsty for blood. My blood.

I break out into a sweat. I never know whether to
creep past or run as fast as I can.

So usually I stand there for ten minutes until my shirt is soaked with sweat. By this time the Beast has smelled me. Anyone within a hundred feet could smell me. The stink of pure terror.

That's when the Beast bounds out and hurls its huge, powerful body at the flimsy fence that separates us.

It is snarling and drooling, crazed for the taste of human flesh. My flesh in particular.

One day, the gate will be left open by mistake.

I'll be mincemeat.

The Beast is bad. But things get worse when I reach the schoolyard. That's where I meet the Vampires.

2

The Vampires

There are three of them. Their skin is deathly white, their lips a livid, bloodstained red. I can see the gore of the poor victims before me still dripping from their fangs.

"Your money or your blood," they screech.

I know they'd just love me to refuse to hand
over my money, so they could drain my poor
body dry, kick it, and throw it in the gutter.

That's what they've done to other kids — I know.
I've seen the zombies who wander around this
school. You can tell when you look in their eyes.
Not a spark of life.

Better to be hungry, thin, and alive, than try to
battle the forces of evil single-handed and end
up a zonked-out zombie. I hand over my money.
As quick as I can.

Now, you might think when I get into school,
I will be safe. No way. The Crazed Wild Beast
and the Blood-sucking Vampires are just small
problems compared to my teacher.

3

The Tyrannosaurus

You wouldn't think my teacher could be a Tyrannosaurus if you came into our class at a good time. First thing in the morning, for instance, Ms. Regina is full of smiles and jokes.

As the morning wears on, little things start to go wrong.

It might start when she is telling us a story. She's great at stories, and she'll just be getting to the really exciting bit. We're all sitting there, rapt, except for Jake who's poking Simon in the ear and Ben who's gluing Helen's pigtail to the desk.

Then comes the warning crackle on the intercom.

"Sorry to disturb you, Ms. Regina, but could you please send the following children to the principal's office: Sally Davies; Ben Michaels; mumble mumble; mumble mumble; Samuel Lei; Sharon Tucker; and mumble mumble."

Of course, half-a-dozen kids (those who know they didn't do anything bad and just want to see what's going on and kiss up) say their names were part of the mumble mumble. Sharon Tucker and Ben Michaels say they didn't hear their names at all, and Ben adds he'll kick out the teeth of any kids who say they did.

Ms. Regina has to send two people to the office for a written list, and cope with Sharon Tucker bursting into tears and trying to hide under a table.

While Ms. Regina's on the floor trying to comfort Sharon, Ben starts trying to kick out teeth.

Before long, half the class is at the principal's office, and the book Ms. Regina was reading to us has been lost in the scuffle.

This teacher doesn't smile so much now.

I can just feel the pressure building.
I know it won't take much for IT to happen.

So when Damien puts the trash can on his head
and leaves a trail of pencil sharpenings, dirty
tissues, and banana peel around the room,
I put my head down on my desk, and wait.

Trembling.

First comes the roar. The windows shake.
Ms. Regina's hair stands up straight, then it
swirls down and molds into her head.

Her face twists, and her body swells with an
awful rippling sound. Her skin breaks out in
scaly lumps.

Her arms shrivel, and long sharp claws shoot out of the ends of her toes. And her teeth. Her teeth are the worst thing — jagged and piercing enough to take off a limb with one bite.

Then Ms. Regina roars again and stomps up and down the room with a murderous gleam in her eye.

Yes, my teacher turns into a Tyrannosaurus.

I just sit there, staring at my desk, praying for the earth to swallow me up. I mean, wouldn't you rather sink down into the magma than be slowly devoured by a prehistoric monster?

She hasn't devoured me yet. So far I've been lucky. I've decided not to go to school anymore.

4

Rebellion!

You would think that any parent who imagines herself to be kind and loving couldn't possibly send her poor child into the jaws of death to face wild Beasts, Vampires, and Tyrannosauruses.

My mom could.

"I'm not going back to that school," I say firmly, from under the bed.

"Oh yes, you are," says Mom, even more firmly. "*Your* biggest problem is your imagination."

"So now I'm not allowed to have an imagination?"

"You are allowed to have an imagination," says Mom, "after school. Right now I want you DRESSED IN FIVE MINUTES!"

She grabs my big toe and drags me out from under the bed. Very painful.

I start to get out my clothes. Then, as soon as Mom goes out, I zoom out of the bedroom and jump into the laundry basket. (We have a big laundry basket.) I've only just closed the lid when it opens again, and a pile of smelly socks lands on my head.

"Aw, yuk, Dad!" I yell.

"Aw, yuk, yourself," he says. "*What* are you doing in the laundry basket? Out. NOW!"

I get out pretty quick. Dad's not bad at dinosaur impressions himself, especially when he hasn't had his morning coffee.

As soon as he is out of sight, I duck into the linen cupboard. If you wriggle in behind the towels, you can hide quite well, even with the door open a crack.

No luck today. I'm no sooner in there than
Patty opens the door to grab a towel.
She grabs my leg instead and screams.

"Okay, okay," I scream back. "It's only me,
not the local meat-eating monster."

"*You* deserve to be dead meat, you little toad!"
says Patty.

Then she gives me The Look, and yells, "Mom!
Matthew's in the linen cupboard again!
He's making footprints on the towels!"

I make a break for the kitchen. I'm in luck.
It's empty. I'm just trying to squeeze in between
the side of the fridge and the ironing board when
Grandma comes in.

"Not much room to hide in there, Matthew," she says.

I squeeze back out and collapse at the table, head down.

But I'm not beaten yet. I'll just sit right here. I won't move. No one can make me.

5

Plotting and Planning

"If they want me to go to school, they'll just have to drag me every step of the way," I tell Grandma. "Then they'll have to lock the classroom door, because as soon as they let go, I'll run back here as fast as I can."

I wait for Grandma to call Mom and Dad to start the dragging. She doesn't. She sits down next to me and puts her hand on my arm.

"It sounds like you're not very happy at school, Matthew," she says.

The understatement of the year. I run through the whole story again with a few extra bits about bloodcurdling screams and sheer, stark terror.

"It's all true," I say. "At least it *feels* true."

I wait for Grandma to tell me about the problem with my imagination. She doesn't.

"When I was a child, there was a fire-breathing dragon on our street," she says.

"Wow!" I say.

"There were Wicked Werewolves in the playground."

"Double wow!" I say.

"And often our teacher would turn into a Ferocious Fiend who spat fire and brimstone."

"Triple wow with a cherry on the top. I wish I'd thought of that one," I say.

"Well, what did you do?" I ask. "I bet you just never went back, like me."

"Do you really think so?" she says. "Do I look like that kind of person to you?"

I don't know what "that kind of person" looks like (unless it's like me, and Grandma *does* kind of look like me), so I just say, "No, Grandma."

"No," says Grandma. "Although I did think about it. Then my Auntie Joan and I worked out a plan. A plan for each of my huge problems. A plan to cut them down to size. A plan to build me up. That's what you need. A plan. Or three."

PLAN 1 x

Grandma and I work out a plan. Three cutting-down and building-up plans. It's lucky that Grandma has done this before, so we can work them out quickly. Mom and Dad and Patty are busy ganging up to throw me out into the cruel world, plan or no plan.

6

Bringing Down the Beast

So, here I am now, out in the cruel world, armed only with three flimsy plans. I breathe deeply. There's the Beast, head up, on the veranda of the House of Horrors, watching me.

I lean forward a bit to check that the gate is shut. It is. No point in starting off by becoming pet food. Remember, I tell myself, that the Beast cannot actually *get out*.

I look straight at the Beast, then start walking as though I own the footpath. Well, I *do* own it, at least as much as the Beast. No creeping, no running.

This takes the Beast by surprise. It just stays, dumbstruck, on the veranda.

I'm nearly halfway there. Wow, I think, this is easy. Even Grandma didn't think it would be as easy as this.

That's when the Beast gets over the surprise.
To make up for lost time, it leaps off the
veranda and clears the yard in a single bound.
It launches itself at the fence, snarling and
slobbering. The fence trembles — but holds.

I want to run.

I want to cry.

But this is the important bit.

By an enormous effort of will, I stop.

I turn to face this horrible, crazed creature.
I look straight into its rolling, bloodshot eyes.
"Sit," I say in a loud, firm voice. "Bad dog.
Sit!" Then I turn and walk on.

It only stops for a moment, in shock, then starts again, as fierce as ever. But somehow I feel better.

And when I look back, what I see looks less like a Brutal Beast, and more like a middle-sized black dog, just barking.

Nothing to worry about, really.
I mean, what's a barking dog when there are
Vampires ahead? Vampires are a *real* problem.

7

Vanquishing the Vampires

I stop at the last corner before the school and wait. Pretty soon, along comes Stephen from fourth grade. I tell him my plan. He waits, too.

We wait for more kids to arrive. A bunch of kids. An *army* of kids. My plan is *our* plan now. Those Vampires don't stand a chance.

We all charge around the corner together.
An army of Vampire-fighters.

The Vampires are there, waiting for single,
solitary victims. Their jaws drop open, their
fangs hang out, when they see all of us charging
down on them together. They turn and run.
"After them!" I yell.

I'm just about to grab the slowest one when
Mr. Bell, the principal, comes out.

"Stop!" he yells. "What's going on here?
Why are you all chasing these three boys?"

Uh-oh, I think. Here's where *we* get into trouble
for saving ourselves from a grisly end. But
instead Mr. Bell turns to the Vampires.

"*What* have you three been up to now?
I'll see you in my office. The rest of you —
go to your classes."

A funny thing about Vampires. When you see them running away, they lose all their powerful vampirish looks. They just look like scared kids. And why should I worry about scared kids? Me, who's got to go into class with a Tyrannosaurus?

Now, that's a *real* problem.

8

Triumph Over Terror

At first, it looks like I won't need Plan 3 today.

Things are going well for Ms. Regina. We are all busy working on the display about recycling for the local shopping center.

We've made signs and posters with photographs and paintings. We've nearly finished.

Our work looks great. The best bit is the huge collection of recyclable junk formed into the shape of the recycling symbol. It stands on its own at the front.

"A symbol of our society," Ms. Regina says.

I'm just helping stick a couple more scraps of paper on one of the arrows, when June says, "I feel sick."

Ten seconds later, and you've guessed it, recycled Coco Pops and orange juice all over the recycling symbol.

Ms. Regina is quite good about it, really.

She gets Jannelle to take June to the nurse's office. She fetches a mop and bucket and tries to clean up as much of the sculpture as she can. She even makes jokes about recycling the recycling symbol.

But I can see she's shaken.

And that's when Jade decides to let out the class mouse, Terminator.

Terminator heads for the door. Marion leaps to catch him, and, crash, over goes the display board.

"Ignore the mouse!" yells Ms. Regina.

But what self-respecting kid could ignore an escaping mouse?

Terminator rushes around the edge of the display board, and up the leg of the easel. Shane dives at the easel. The legs of the easel collapse, and the paint jars that were on top of it sail into the air.

It's amazing how three paint jars that were right next to each other can take such different paths. The red lands, splatt! on the display board.

The blue spatters all over the recycling sculpture. It kind of mixes in with the traces of vomit. The green does a double-somersault-twist, and lands on Ms. Regina's head.

The complete silence in the classroom is
shattered by Ms. Regina's roar. The windows
rattle.

The green paint dripping all over its head makes the Tyrannosaurus's swelling and rippling skin look even more hideous than ever before.

Out shoot the hooked, spiky claws.

Those terrible teeth, ready to rip and tear and devour, gnash together wildly.

Its awful bulk looms over me, bursting with savage fury.

But I keep looking at the Tyrannosaurus.

I don't put my head on my desk. I don't wait for the earth to swallow me up.

I remember what Grandma said.

"Think about it," were her words. "Has the Tyrannosaurus ever really attacked anyone? It's all noise and fury. You're safe. Think about it. And look at it."

So I grit my teeth. I hold my breath. And I look at it.

First I open my eyes a little, tiny bit.

Then wider. And wider.

There it is. A quite spectacular Tyrannosaurus.

Almost... a *wonderfully* terrifying Tyrannosaurus.

A kind of... *excitingly* scarifying Tyrannosaurus.

And now that I *really* look at it, I think I can even see someone a bit like Ms. Regina in there somewhere.

It's hard to tell under all that green paint.